WHERE THE WILD MUMS ARE

For my mum, with thanks, now that I understand.
K. B.

To Jenny and for all the Wild Mums everywhere.
S. W.

First published in the UK in 2015
by Faber and Faber Limited
Bloomsbury House,
74–77 Great Russell Street, London WC1B 3DA

Text copyright © Katie Blackburn, 2015
Illustration copyright © Sholto Walker, 2015

ISBN 978-0-571-32151-3

Printed in China.

3 5 7 9 10 8 6 4 2

WHERE THE WILD MUMS ARE

Written by
KATIE BLACKBURN

Illustrated by
SHOLTO WALKER

FABER & FABER

The day Mum didn't get dressed and went on strike,

Dad called her A Wild Thing

and Mum said, 'Cook your *own* dinner,'
and stomped off upstairs to run a bath.

That evening, as Mum lay in her bathtub,
a paradise wove itself all around her

until the entire bathroom was hung with wild fruits
and the walls themselves seemed to fade and disappear.

The air was full of promise and
waves softly lapped the shore.

A yacht lay on the sands
and Mum stepped into it
and floated away across time and space

until she came to the place
where the Wild Mums are . . .

And when the Wild Mums saw her,
they shook their magnificent heads and wiggled their magnificent
hips and stamped their magnificent feet.

But Mum just laughed, and danced as though there were no end to her wildness and magnificence,

all the while balancing a drink on her head and not spilling it, and they were dazzled and said she should be Queen of the Wild Mums.

And Mum said – 'I accept.
Now let's get this party started!'

And there was never a wild magnificence like it.

Until –
'Enough!' Mum cried.
For the Queen of the Wild Mums suddenly felt a little bit tired and emotional and wished she were with those she loved more than anything in the world.

At that very moment from miles away across the waters,
as if by magic, Mum could tell that she was needed.

So she stopped being
Queen of the Wild Mums.

'Oh stay a little longer,'
the Wild Mums wailed,
'we're having such fun,
come join the conga,'
but Mum just smiled.

She stepped into her yacht
and floated across time and space
back into the waters of her very own bathtub.

There was a cup of
tea waiting for her.

It was all right.

She was home.